DATE DUE

DEMCO 38-297

The World of Fashion

Fashion TRENDS

How Popular Style Is Shaped

by Jen Jones

Consultant: Lindsay Stewart
Director of the Children's Division
Jet Set Models
La Jolla, California

Capstone press®
Mankato, Minnesota

Snap Books are published by Capstone Press,

151 Good Counsel Drive, P.O. Box 669, Mankato, Minnesota 56002.

www.capstonepress.com

Library of Congress Cataloging-in-Publication Data

Jones, Jen, 1976–

Fashion trends : how popular style is shaped / by Jen Jones.

p. cm.—(Snap books. The world of fashion)

Summary: "Explores the world of trends and sales and the roles media and marketing play into fashion trends"—
Provided by publisher.

Includes bibliographical references and index.

ISBN-13: 978-0-7368-6831-0 (hardcover)

ISBN-10: 0-7368-6831-3 (hardcover)

ISBN-13: 978-0-7368-7885-2 (softcover pbk.)

ISBN-10: 0-7368-7885-8 (softcover pbk.)

1. Fashion—Juvenile literature. 2. Clothing and dress—Juvenile literature. 3. Women's clothing—Juvenile literature
I. Title. II. Series.

TT515.J59 2007

746.9'2—dc22   2006021846

Editor: Amber Bannerman

Designer: Juliette Peters

Photo Researcher: Charlene Deyle

Photo Credits:

AP/Wide World Photos/Women's Wear Daily, George Chinsee, 25; Capstone Press/Karon Dubke, 14, 17 (both), 23; Corbis/
New York Newswire/Steve Sands, 9; Corbis/Peter M. Fisher, 27; Corbis/Roger Ressmeyer, 29 (left); Corbis/zefa/A.B./Holger
Winkler, 21; Corbis/zefa/Gulliver, 29 (right); Getty Images Inc./Getty Images Publicity, 13; Getty Images Inc./Iconica/
Simon Wilkinson, 15; Getty Images Inc./Mark Mainz, 10; Getty Images Inc./NBC Television, 11; Getty Images Inc./
Photonica/LaCoppola-Meier, cover; Getty Images Inc./The Image Bank/David Sacks, 6; Getty Images Inc./The Image Bank/
Stuart O'Sullivan, 5; Michele Torma Lee, 32; PhotoEdit Inc./Bill Aron, 18; Shutterstock/C Salisbury, 28; Shutterstock/Chin
Kit Sen, 20; Shutterstock/ErickN, 8; Shutterstock/Jeff Gynane, 16; Shutterstock/Ken Hurst, 19 (TV); Shutterstock/Orla, 19
(runners); Shutterstock/Rick Orrell, cover; Shutterstock/Melissa King, 24; Shutterstock/Scott Maxwell, 26

1 2 3 4 5 6 12 11 10 09 08 07

Table of Contents

Introduction

What Is a Trend? 4

Chapter One

What's Hot, What's Not? Who Decides? 6

Chapter Two

Media, Marketing, and the Mind:

Outside Influence on Trends 14

Chapter Three

Consumer Culture: Its Powerful Pulse 22

Glossary 30

Fast Facts 30

Read More 31

Internet Sites 31

About the Author 32

Index 32

What Is a Trend?

Take a look through your closet. The clothes inside probably fit into two categories: timeless or trendy. That little black dress? Timeless. That sequined skirt? Trendy.

A timeless piece never goes out of style. A trendy look is popular yet short-lived. People who dress to impress are often the first to show off new clothing trends. But it's hard to keep up with the fast-paced fashion industry. A formerly fabulous fad can become "so yesterday" in the blink of an eye.

In this book, we'll dig beneath the surface. We'll look at how trends form and the media's role in the fashion industry. You'll also learn how to be a smarter consumer and how to develop your own style.

Chapter One

What's Hot, What's Not? Who Decides?

Purses and shoes and cute shirts, oh my! There is no shortage of ways for teens to spend money. Nowhere is that fact more evident than at the mall. There you'll find tons of teens indulging their passion for fashion.

Clothing companies know that teens pack a powerful spending punch. They spend about $2 billion per year on advertising to tweens and teens. By creating eye-catching ads and trendy apparel, each company competes to snag the youth market's attention. Tweens and teens are most definitely the kings and queens of cool!

Teen Magnets

A growing number of clothing companies are building their businesses around attracting young people. Among them are stores like:

- Abercrombie & Fitch

- American Eagle Outfitters

- Forever 21

- Hot Topic

- Rampage

- Torrid

- Wet Seal

Designers with Impact

Fashion designers try to design products that teens will love. What's your designer IQ? If you can spot a Dooney & Bourke purse by its logo, you probably know your fashion stuff. But why is it so important to some people to show off items by famous designers?

For some, it's about status. They know others who see their Coach bag will know it was expensive. Certain designer labels are very popular with tweens and teens. Juicy Couture is known for youthful, colorful clothing. Tommy Hilfiger's line is clean-cut and stylish.

When shopping, remember that designer clothes cost more than most. Do you have a hard time deciding between a jacket that costs $25 and one that costs $80? If you do, think about all the things you could buy with the extra $55! Is it worth it to shell out extra money just for a label?

Tommy Hilfiger with two models at one of his fashion shows

The Birth of a Trend

The life cycle of a trend is like a domino effect. One domino starts the movement. It doesn't stop until all the dominoes have fallen over. When you notice sequin purses everywhere you look, you've spotted a new fashion trend.

Celebrities play a big part in trendsetting. The general public copies their looks in hopes of having the same appeal. Do you remember when Mary-Kate Olsen started dressing in a bohemian style? Soon, teens everywhere adopted her "boho chic" look. In the 1990s, Jennifer Aniston showed off a new hairstyle on *Friends*. That hairstyle was soon copied by millions!

"Boho chic"
Mary-Kate Olsen

Jennifer Aniston with her '90s hairstyle

Of course, non-celebrities can also spark new trends. A small group of fashion-forward leaders acts as the domino for a larger group of followers. Their courage to wear something different sets the mainstream pace. As more people start wearing the new style, the buying public puts the product in high demand. At this point, the leaders look for something fresh to set themselves apart. The trend cycle begins again!

Seasons Change

Just as the weather changes, so do the fashions of the moment. In fact, the fashion world has its own set of seasons. Designers usually debut clothes at runway shows during fall and spring. At these glamorous events, the audience gets a sneak peek at new fashions.

The industry's idea of what's "hot" and "not" can shift rapidly. Flowing gaucho pants may be popular one season. The next season might be all about capri pants. About every ten years, society goes through a major shift in trends. For example, the '80s were all about bright, crazy clothing. The '90s were marked by grungy flannels and ripped jeans.

Of course, not all trends flatter every body type or person. You have the power to choose the right pieces for you. There's no need to follow every fashion trend!

Chapter Two

Media, Marketing, and the Mind: Outside Influence on Trends

Youthful magazines have popped up as little sisters to magazines like *Vogue* and *Elle*. Why the sudden onset of teen fashion magazines? It's simple. Young new clothes addicts are hungry for the latest news and trends. In magazines like *Cosmo! Girl*, readers can learn about new designers and check out budget-friendly versions of Hollywood's trends.

You might not guess that many magazines have hidden advertorials. These ads are disguised as stories. Companies pay magazines big bucks to cover their products in this way.

The idea behind an advertorial is that if it looks like a story, the reader won't be as likely to turn the page. So next time you read a blurb about snag-free tights, know that the magazine might be pushing the product. Make buying decisions based on your likes and budget, and you won't go wrong!

Marketing by Mail

After the Internet's rise, some experts predicted
mail catalogs would go the way of the dinosaur. Yet
companies still use mail-order marketing to reach
tweens and teens. A catalog's design says a lot about
the market the company is trying to reach. For
instance, the dELiA*s catalog shows clean-cut kids in
casual or sporty settings. The Urban Outfitters catalog
has more of a hip, artsy look, and shows teens out
and about.

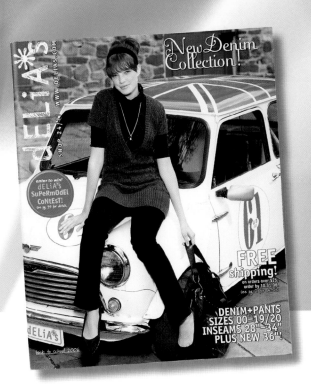

What sets one catalog apart from the rest? Catalogs often have festive themes like "Summer Fun" or "Back-to-School." Lots of money is spent to send photographers and models to beautiful locations. These places provide the best backdrop for the clothing. But in trying to capture attention, some companies cross the line. In 2003, Abercrombie & Fitch had to pull its catalog after parents complained about its edgy, racy pictures.

Ad Wizards at Work

From blinking Internet banners to glossy magazine ads, advertisements are part of everyday life. By the time a girl turns 17, she will have seen more than 250,000 commercials. Whether watching TV or listening to the radio, ads are hard to escape.

When designing an ad campaign, companies choose a target audience for their message. After selecting a group like "Teens" or "Dads," an ad is created to play on their particular needs and wants. For example, a sportswear ad geared at tweens and teens might show attractive girls running in a race. Whether this ad "scores" with real teens is something only *you* can decide!

Signs of an Effective Ad

Will an ad hit a home run with its target audience? To do so, it must:

- Tie an image or emotion to the brand.

- Hint at the type of person who might enjoy the product.

- Make a convincing case that a product is worth buying.

The In "Click"

Gone are the days of going only to the mall for your fashion fix. Now shopping is as easy as a click of the mouse. In 2005, young Internet surfers spent more than $10 billion shopping on sites like gojane.com and daisymaze.com.

The Internet also makes it easy for teens to follow trends. On fashion blogs and message boards, teens can discuss what's "in" and "out." They can give advice on what to wear on the first day of school or to the big dance.

Young people can also show off their own personal style on Web sites. MySpace profiles can be decorated with custom layouts by clothing lines like Roxy and Louis Vuitton. On sites like TheFashionSpot.com and The-N.com, users can dress up images of themselves in different outfits. With such great and easy ways to do fashion experiments, new trends are sure to take shape.

Chapter Three

Consumer Culture: Its Powerful Pulse

To keep up with changing trends, designers must always look for "the next big thing." That's why clothing companies hire specific employees to predict popular items coming down the pike.

Numerous companies exist solely to find out what young people like and dislike. Girls' Intelligence Agency has recruited 40,000 girls who act as "secret agents" and weigh in with their own views. A company called Look-Look sniffs out new trends by doing polls with people on the street and conducting focus groups. Then the company tries to guess how new products will be received.

"Baby" from Dirty Dancing *in her rolled shorts*

Staying current on what's hot in entertainment is another way to predict fashion trends. If a movie is number one at the box office, millions of viewers have seen it. When *Dirty Dancing* became a blockbuster hit in the 1980s, girls everywhere started wearing rolled shorts like the main character, "Baby." When Britney Spears first hit the scene in 1999, her brand of schoolgirl chic became all the rage.

The Right Place, the Right Time

   We live in a high-tech world. Viewers can
fast-forward commercials and click off pop-up ads.
This technology has forced companies to find new ways
to reach consumers. One popular and less obvious
method is product placement. When your favorite TV
character wears a Fubu jacket or sports a Nike hat,
you're seeing product placement at work.

Gwen Stefani shows off her L.A.M.B. clothing line.

In the fashion world, product placement often goes hand in hand with Hollywood. As stars walk the red carpet, reporters ask what designer they're "wearing." Everyone at home then hears the mention of Chanel or Christian Dior. Some celebrities even try to promote their own clothing lines. Sean "Diddy" Combs has worn his line of Sean John clothes on MTV. Gwen Stefani has worn her clothing line, L.A.M.B., to events.

25

Money, Money, Money

In the business world, everything comes down to the "bottom line," or how much money a company makes. No doubt fashion is a booming industry. In 2005, clothing sales in the U.S. reached more than $181 billion! With so much money at stake, companies must aggressively compete for customers. And when competition heats up, more and more catchy marketing ideas come into play.

Today's society is very much focused on material things. Many people spend rather than save money. Unlike adults who have bills to pay, most tweens and teens can spend money as they wish. This fact hasn't escaped clothing companies, who invest time and big money to attract your attention.

To avoid wasting your money, take some time
to think before buying a product you want. If it's a
trendy item, it may be out of style soon. Will it fit
your personal style long after it's *out* of style? Can you
afford it? If a few days go by and you feel confident
that it's a smart buy, go for it!

The Culture of "Cool"

Looking at fad fashions from the past, one question comes to mind—"What were they *thinking*?" Through the years, popular ideas about what's "cool" have driven people to don neon T-shirts and tease their hair to horrifying heights. Back in the day, your parents probably wore bellbottoms or Zubaz. We've all fallen victim to an embarrassing trend at some point!

1980s fashion

Trends of today

The reason we buy into silly fads boils down to a need to belong. Sometimes we think that people will accept us more if we look like everyone else. Though it is great to follow fashion, it's more important to come up with your own personal style. Looking the way others think you should look keeps you from growing into who you really are. Daring to be different is the mark of a *true* trendsetter.

Glossary

advertisement (AD-ver-tize-muhnt)— a public notice, usually published in the press or broadcast over the air, that calls attention to a product

blog (BLOG)—an online journal, short for weblog

campaign (kam-PAYN)—an organized effort

consumer (kuhn-SOO-mur)— a member of the buying public

debut (DAY-byu)—a first appearance

logo (LOH-goh)—a visual symbol for a company

marketing (MAR-ke-ting)—methods used by a company to convince people to buy its products

Fast Facts

In the 1960s, fashion-forward First Lady Jackie Kennedy set off many a fashion trend. Women everywhere copied her love of pillbox hats. These small circular hats covered just the top of women's heads.

Who knew a simple ring could tip you off to someone's mood? In the 1970s, mood rings were all the rage. In theory, they changed color according to a person's current mood.

Hypercolor shirts are among the tackiest trends of the 1980s. The shirts were made of fabric that responded to body heat. Breathing on them or leaving a handprint on them would cause them to change colors!

Read More

Desetta, Al. *The Courage to Be Yourself: True Stories By Teens About Cliques, Conflicts, and Overcoming Peer Pressure.* Minneapolis: Free Spirit Publishing, 2005.

Marron, Maggie. *Stylin': Great Looks for Teens.* New York: Michael Friedman Publishing Group, 2001.

Muharrar, Aisha. *More Than a Label: Why What You Wear or Who You're With Doesn't Define Who You Are.* Minneapolis: Free Spirit Publishing, 2002.

Internet Sites

FactHound offers a safe, fun way to find Internet sites related to this book. All of the sites on FactHound have been researched by our staff.

Here's how:
1. Visit *www.facthound.com*
2. Choose your grade level.
3. Type in this book ID **0736868313** for age-appropriate sites. You may also browse subjects by clicking on letters, or by clicking on pictures and words.
4. Click on the **Fetch It** button.

FactHound will fetch the best sites for you!

31

About the Author

Jen Jones has always been fascinated by fashion—and the evidence can be found in her piles of magazines and overflowing closet! She is a Los Angeles-based writer who has published stories in magazines such as *American Cheerleader*, *Dance Spirit*, *Ohio Today*, and *Pilates Style*. She has also written for E! Online and PBS Kids. Jones has been a Web site producer for *The Jenny Jones Show*, *The Sharon Osbourne Show*, and *The Larry Elder Show*. She's also written books for young girls on cheerleading, knitting, figure skating, and gymnastics.

Index

ad campaigns, 19
advertisements, 14, 18, 19, 24
advertorials, 14–15

blogs, 20

catalogs, 16, 17
celebrities, 10, 25
commercials, 18, 24
consumers, 5, 24

designer labels, 8
designers, 8, 12, 14, 22, 25

logos, 8

magazines, 14–15, 18
media, 5
message boards, 20
money, 6, 8, 17, 26, 27
movies, 23

product placement, 24–25

runway shows, 12

society, 12, 26

target audience, 19

Web sites, 20–21